ANIMAL KINGDOM

Colouring Book
For Adults

Om Books International

Om Books International

Reprinted in 2022

Corporate & Editorial Office
A-12, Sector 64, Noida 201 301
Uttar Pradesh, India
Phone: +91 120 477 4100
Email: editorial@ombooks.com
Website: www.ombooksinternational.com

Sales Office
107, Ansari Road, Darya Ganj
New Delhi 110 002, India
Phone: +91 11 4000 9000
Email: sales@ombooks.com
Website: www.ombooks.com

ISBN: 978-93-85609-74-9

Printed in India

10 9 8 7 6 5 4 3

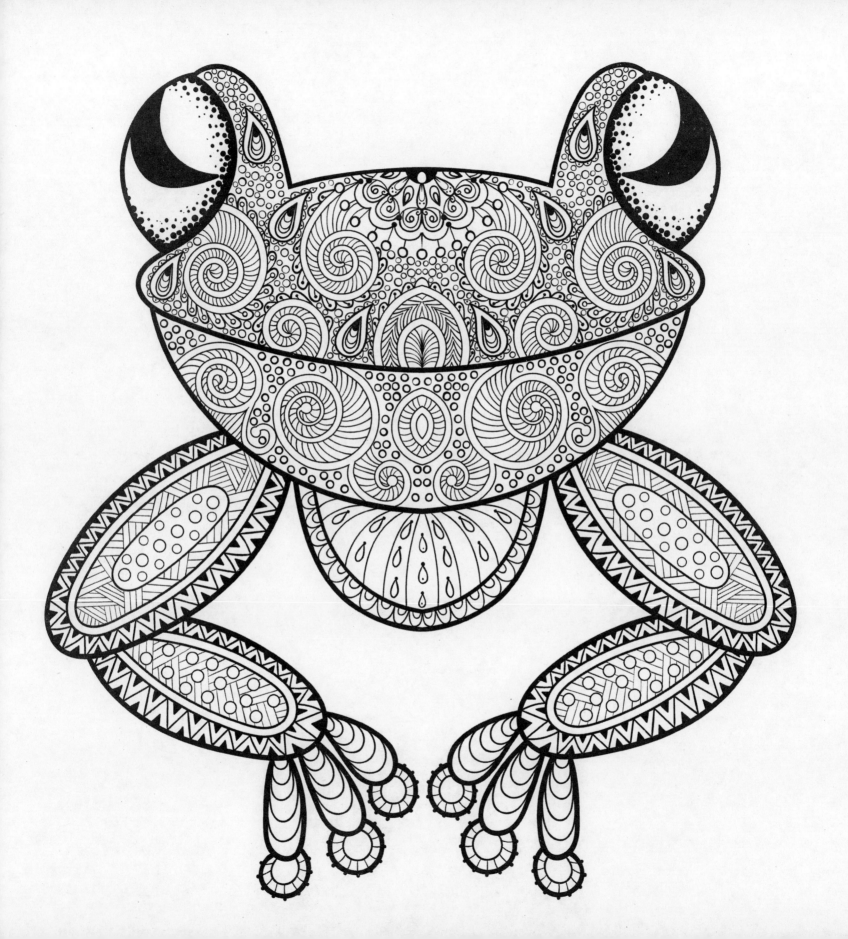

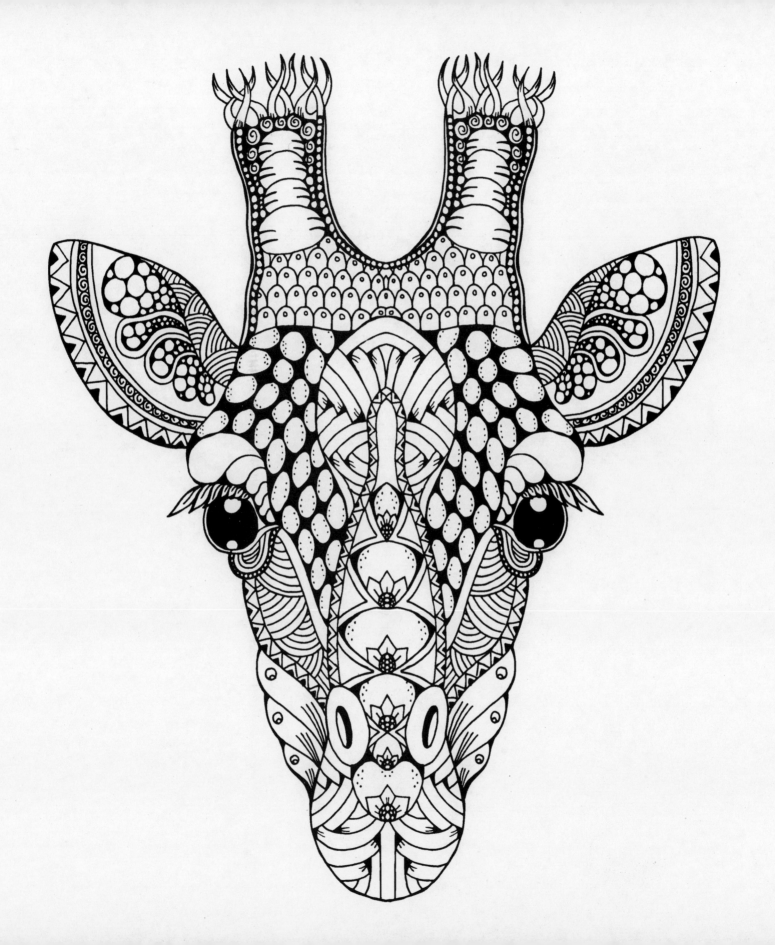